MAIDEN
VOYAGE

LANCE ERLICK

Finlee Augare Books (Chicago)

This is a work of fiction. All of the characters, organizations, and events portrayed herein are either products of the author's imagination or are used fictitiously, and any similarities to actual persons, organizations, or events is entirely coincidental. Also, though locations used in this work exist, for dramatic effect details have been altered. Accordingly, they should be considered fictitious.

Finlee Augare Books, Chicago, IL
ISBN: 978-0-9889968-9-2 (print)
ISBN: 978-0-9914643-3-3 (e-book)

Printed in the United States of America

To my muse

Nina Rekovic Private Log 2098-10-17/8:06 AM

Another security sweep and another boring diversion from my Chief Engineer duties. In the five years since we left Earth's orbit, it's been mostly crimes of boredom: squabbles over limited space and who-did-what-to-or-with-whom.

In the orange com-room I find my sweetie, Chief Communications Officer Carmen Blythe. Her lithe, muscular form jerks to attention when I enter. She's been dozing again: end of shift.

I push aside her brown curls and massage her knotted shoulders. She leans forward to give me room to loosen the muscles across her well-toned back. Being on opposing shifts, I rarely see her, like ghosts passing at twilight. Her shift ends as mine begins. At least I can time my security sweeps to catch her before she gets off. She rises; gives me a welcome hug and a lingering kiss: implied promises for the weekend.

Lucky me, at least I get to move on my rounds. Carmen has to sit and listen to intermittent Earth-coms that now take a year to reach us. The rarely used QE-com light flashes and squawks static that could wake the dead.

Carmen pulls away. "Got-to-go." She looks like she's been studying all night for com finals and needs an adrenaline boost.

I should get on with my rounds, but I linger. It feels good to hang with Carmen and watch her work. She's the reason I signed onto the Maiden's Ark after my dad's prolonged brain cancer got the better of him. He refused advanced treatments; he didn't want to artificially prolong his life.

Quantum-Entanglement-coms are unusual. To provide their limited instantaneous communications, Captain Belova McDaniels—I call her Beluga because of her size—installed two QE containment units. The first entangles with a sister unit in Colorado Springs; the other on the miss-named 'dark' side of the moon, the side facing away from Earth.

Carmen runs the QE signal through filters to verify consistency and reconstruct the message from the few bits of transmitted data. This much I've gathered from scattered weekend conversations over drinks. She has to tease out the message before its delicate quantum bits are lost.

I tremble with excitement. The last QE-com two years ago announced election results: Neanderthals won. Actually, real Neanderthals would have been an improvement. The election only reinforced Captain McDaniel's rationale for leaving the Earth behind and starting a new life.

Of course it took over seven months for the regular Earth-com details to arrive. The Radical Patriot's Party had won by promising to gut the space budget as they took a machete to all "non-essential" government programs.

Three words scroll across Carmen's screen:
Earth lost asteroid.

"What does it mean?" I ask. Mention of asteroids triggers memories of my ex-boyfriend and his asteroid mining operations, which were more important to him than I was. Carmen helped me pick up the pieces when he left one day without saying goodbye.

She looks up as if she just notices me. "They lost an

asteroid? Why send that message?"

"That's it?"

Carmen shakes her head while probing the message. "The rest is ... gibberish." She works frantically at her controls. "Not good. The helium atoms split."

I shut up, let her concentrate, and try to make sense of the cryptic message and how unnerved Carmen is. I've never seen her so anxious. I hold my breath until she finishes. When she pushes away from the controls, she digs her fingers into her scalp, grabbing clumps of brown hair. I try to hold her, but she pulls away and does a mad crazy dance in the middle of the orange com-room. She's hyperventilating and yet her tan skin has gone pale.

"What is it, Hon?"

She catches her breath. "Earth's gone! Has to be."

Carmen spins around as if searching for her anchor, but when I approach, she pushes me away. Eyes narrow; she regains focus. "It would take a nuke to split helium like that. I had to jettison the QE-unit before the containment field collapsed and destroyed our ship."

"We can't communicate with Earth anymore?"

"I don't think there's an Earth to communicate with."

"What about the moon base?" I ask.

Carmen drops into her seat and activates the moon's QE-com. I don't want to wait the year it will take for regular electromagnetic signals to reach our Earth-com to confirm what happened. How is this even possible?

I struggle to breathe. I knew signing onto the Maiden's Ark meant never returning to Earth, never being able to visit Dad's grave again. But the thought that his grave might be gone slams my gut, sending its contents in both directions. I steady myself to control the urges.

"This'll take time," Carmen says. "Assuming moon folk are even watching after what happened."

Focus, I tell myself. *I'm Chief of Security.* "We have to tell the captain and the passengers."

Carmen gets up and blocks the door. Her hazel eyes

3

narrow, while her voice descends into a harsh whisper. "Tell no one. Nod that you understand."

I back away. "What's going on? People deserve to know."

"Know what? That we got a garbled message?"

"You said—"

"Keep your mouth shut," Carmen says. "You weren't even supposed to be here."

"Captain McDaniels named me Chief of Security." I almost say Beluga because after years under her thumb, I can't stand our big-boned leader.

Carmen's face softens. When she moves aside, Beluga fills the doorway. I hold my tongue and look up into her dark eyes, which don't meet mine. While I support the captain's mission to start a new civilization with only women, I have growing reservations over her dictatorship. The Maiden's Ark Covenant gives us no recourse. I swallow my reservations and step back.

She enters and closes the door. "Show me the message."

Earth lost asteroid scrolls across the screen.

"Erase it," the captain says.

I interrupt, "Shouldn't we let the crew and passengers—"

"We're not stirring things up for a cryptic message we can't verify for a year. Besides, there's nothing we can do."

"What if survivors need our help?" I ask.

"We don't change plans based on garbled messages. We don't even know if there are survivors. We'll wait until regular channels come through."

"That'll take over a year."

"So be it. Earth's catastrophe, if that's what it is, makes our mission even more critical."

I want to say more, but Carmen's eyes narrow: *shut up.* I nod, though I'm not okay with this. For all I know, the women on board the Maiden's Ark may be all that remain of the human race.

The last regular Earth-com I know of came in yesterday, sent a year ago. It sounded desperate: riots, famine, terror attacks. It was enough to make me glad I'd left. Yet I feel an ache to return and do whatever's possible to help out. Now all our petty squabbles seemed just that—petty.

But Carmen isn't supposed to share Earth-coms with me, so I don't say anything. I don't want the captain mad at her.

The captain turns to me. "Aren't you late for your rounds? You're not on holiday."

I nod, and reach for the door.

Beluga grabs my wrist. "Not a word to anyone."

* * *

Nina Rekovic Private Log 2098-10-17/9:56 AM

The Maiden's Ark with its quarter million women and girls is like a huge high school. Fifty deck levels spread out with twenty-five hundred apartments on each level in a grid of fifty by fifty. I cover some twenty miles of teal-tinted residential corridors using my implanted Eye-pad viewer while I head to the yellow commons on deck fifty, with its stores, exercise facilities, and cafeteria. If I'm going to play cop, might as well have my mid-morning donut—a soy-algae substitute that tries. At least it's not fattening. I don't need Carmen getting on my case.

Our Chief Cook, olive-skinned Francesca Giovanni, greets me with a tray of my favorites. They all taste the same. She makes an effort by giving these a floral rainbow coloring—natural algae tones, of course.

"You look like end of shift," Francesca says. "You up all night?"

I shake my head. "Focused on my Eye-pad too long."

She laughs.

It takes all my self-control not to tell Francesca what I've learned. I need to tell someone. To let out this ache inside me that there's really no going back. I pray for some other explanation, but Carmen was definite. One of our

QE-coms is gone, severed forever. I steel my nerves—can't let on.

Unlike me, Francesca left people behind and regrets "getting tricked" into signing on. When she broke up with her philandering husband, one of Beluga's faithful befriended her. Like joining a religious cult Francesca got all the surround-love she needed. Before she knew it, she was on the Maiden's Ark.

Now she's one of the Returners who want to turn this ship around and go home. She wasn't one of the twelve who signed the petition four years ago and spent six months in lockup. There were many like her who sympathized, but refused to sign. Some of Maiden's Ark most devout colonists said we should pack all the Returners on a shuttle and send them back, but with insufficient supplies: a death sentence. Thankfully Beluga didn't agree, though I suspect she didn't want to lose one of her shuttles.

I can't say I blame the Returners. At twenty percent of light speed, we don't expect to reach the blue-green planet QX-22864 for another hundred-and-twenty years. By that time most of us who began this journey will be dead. This was all in the fine print.

"No chance of turning this boat around is there?" she asks for the thousandth time.

I force a smile. *Yeah, but I can't tell you unless I want to spend six months recycling human waste down in lockup.*

"No disturbances this morning?" I ask.

"The usual: two restless girls started a food fight, three teens complained about bland food. I do my best."

"I know you do. You want me to investigate?"

"I took care of it. Get your head back into engineering, where you belong."

She knows I don't like security. I make my way down the lift to engineering on level fourteen, eating the soy-algae pastries on the way. At the same time, I scan all the common areas on other levels on my Eye-pad. While I don't see anything to worry about, many of these women would be upset if they knew. Captain Beluga is right. Why get them riled up when there's nothing they can do. We'll keep getting messages for another year. Then we'll have real answers.

When I reach the white hallway lined with engineering rooms, I bump into my blonde Senior Engineer Zola Cohen. I offer her the remaining donut. I want to tell her what happened to her family on Earth, for the sake of her and her reclusive teenage daughter Magdalena, but her pinched face seems intent on something else.

"Problems?" I ask.

"Nothing I can't handle. I left reports on your desk."

I want to ask why she didn't forward them to my Eye-pad, but she hurries down the sterile corridor. I move to my desk and go through the usual problems: damage to a forward shield, clogged air-cleansing unit, adjustments to recycling tanks. When Captain Beluga named me Chief of Security, I put Zola in charge of engineering during my absences. She's done fine without me.

I guess I'm expendable.

* * *

Nina Rekovic Private Log 2098-10-17/4:43 PM

Tired of reports and budgets, I start my afternoon security sweep by checking on the whereabouts of my sweetie. I want to see her, but I also want to know what the moon's QE-com revealed. I locate Carmen entering Captain Beluga's office, yuck. In fairness, the captain isn't ugly. She's just bigger than most women, and has a commanding voice and intimidating personality. She also has the Covenant making her Empress of this realm.

After scanning residential corridors and commons, nothing concerning, I stop off at the darkened observation lounge on forty-nine. Two couples are making out under the stars. It makes me think of Carmen, though she doesn't like public displays of affection. I finish my rounds and find her in the blue wing on forty-nine, sitting at the bar with two of her com techies. They're all dressed in floral leisure gowns. She changed. I sit beside her on an elevated seat that adjusts to my height and weight.

She pushes some blue-green concoction my way. "Try it. Something new."

I take a sip; enjoy tingling around my mouth before it goes down. Like all "drinks" on board, the alcohol content is severely limited. It also contains a mild sedative to keep drinkers from getting rowdy. Carmen is already zoning out. She should be catching up on sleep, but the Earth communication must be troubling her.

Wanting answers, I escort her along blue corridors, through the yellow commons, down the lift to seven and along our residential hallway.

"You could have stayed for drinks," Carmen says. "Try to be sociable."

She leans into me until I get her into the apartment. After I open the door, she stumbles into the bedroom and plops onto the bed, fully clothed. I've missed her awake-time. Now it's time for her beauty rest. But if I sleep now, I'll be up during her shift with nothing I want to do.

"Come on, you're not sleeping in your leisure gown."

She gets up. "I don't need a nursemaid." She looks alert; then stumbles to the wall-dresser and stands there.

I steady her. "What was in the moon's QE-com?"

She pulls away. "Lunar confirmed: Two asteroids collided. Debris hit Earth. Coms lost. Volcanic activity. Thick clouds."

"What about our moon colonies?"

"Earth-side gone. Five thousand on far side survived, plus asteroid miners."

"Was this a terrorist attack?"

Carmen shakes her head, her expression grim. "No way to know."

"The lunar colony can't survive without resupply," I say.

"I know. Plus, Earth's orbit may have altered. We're trying to calculate."

"We have to tell the others. We have to go back."

Carmen straightens up as if from a jolt of adrenaline. She places her hand on my cheek, almost a slap. "Tell no one. If this goes public, it'll stir up Returners. We're not going back."

I remove her hand. "What's gotten into you? Survivors will need our help."

"As Chief of Security, your job is to maintain peace, not to stir up trouble."

"Don't lecture me."

Carmen pushes past me. "Don't cross the captain."

"What's that supposed to mean?" I follow her to the door. "And where are you going?"

"Not your concern. Don't follow."

She slips out into the corridor and slams the door.

I want to call her back, but not for another fight. I let her go.

* * *

Nina Rekovic Private Log 2098-10-18/8:18 AM

On my way to visit Carmen in the com-room as part of my morning security sweep, I scan my Eye-pad. On almost every level, small groups whisper in yellow corridors.

Am I being paranoid or has word gotten out?

I shake it off. Common areas attract cliques gossiping about who's sleeping with whom and who did what to their best friend.

When I enter the orange com-room, Carmen isn't happy to see me.

I close the door. "I missed you last night." *A lot.*

Actually, I miss the Carmen I knew on Earth, the one I gave up everything to follow onboard. Back then we had candlelight dinners by the river and took walks. Now all we do is avoid each other and fight. I sigh.

Carmen's hazel eyes narrow as if she doesn't know me.

9

"You had to do it, didn't you?"

"Do what?"

"Who did you tell?"

I back against the wall. "Not a soul."

"Don't tell me you didn't notice Returners gossiping."

"Just the usual."

Captain Beluga enters the com-room without knocking and towers over me. "We have a problem."

"Carmen was briefing me," I say, trying to get in front of her challenge.

The captain frowns, wrinkling her large forehead. She shakes her head. "I just came from the fertility lab. Someone sabotaged our EggFusion apparatus. I don't have to tell you what that means. Or who is responsible."

I struggle to breathe. The future of our all-female society, maybe the entire human race, depends on the success of EggFusion Fertilization, the ability to fertilize one woman's egg with another woman's cells. Without it, we're extinct in a generation. "You think Returners did this?"

"Who else?"

"Couldn't it be a malfunction? I'll get my engineers—"

"Zola's working on it. I want you to round up all Returners for questioning. Quarantine them until I decide how to deal with this."

"We can't—"

"This is a terrorist attack! Under Article Nine, Section Twenty-Three of the Maiden's Ark Covenant, I hereby order you to imprison all suspects, which means all Returners. You may deputize whoever you need to assist. Take them to Deck A."

That's next to recycling.

I look to Carmen who returns to her seat, and another Lunar QE-com.

* * *

Nina Rekovic Private Log 2098-10-18/8:58 AM

I know most of the Returners, having talked them

down from despair. It doesn't seem fair to use that knowledge and confidences against them. Yet someone had jeopardized our future. If I arrest them, I'm a skunk. If I don't, I'm a traitor.

There's nothing in my inbox from Zola, which annoys me. I message her to tell me the instant she learns anything. Then I hurry down yellow corridors to visit Francesca. She greets me with her soy-algae donuts, all smiles. "New flavor today."

I hold up my hands. I can't accept these and then arrest her. "You heard about the fertility lab?"

She drops the donuts on a nearby table. "Terrible business. I hope you catch whoever did this."

I sigh. "Captain's orders. I have to quarantine all Returners."

"I see." Offering no resistance, she holds her hands behind for me to cuff.

"I was hoping you'd help me gather them peacefully. I'd like to deputize you."

"Me?" Francesca says. "I'm just a crotchety old woman, all talk. Are the rumors about Earth true?" She lowers her voice. "Or is that so Returners will stop griping?"

"Francesca, please. I don't want anyone getting hurt. This is serious."

"People trust you. Now you're betraying them?"

"I'm not a priest or a lawyer," I say. "Nothing told to me is privileged, not when it involves the safety of this ship."

"Very well," Francesca says. "But only to make sure no one gets hurt."

We don't even have to go hunting for Returners. Three young women from electronics fabrication join us, still in tight brown work uniforms. "Is it true what they say?" the supervisor asks.

"Was it nuclear war?" the youngest asks.

"Are there any survivors?"

I look up at camera locations and shake my head. "We can't talk here."

I lead the three fabricators toward lifts in the middle of the commons. Francesca joins me. The betrayal tears at my guts. Yet the last thing I want is rebellion on this fragile vessel, our entire world.

"We're going back for survivors, aren't we?" the youngest fabricator asks.

Two seamstresses from the clothing shop join us as we enter the lift. "Tell us it isn't true," one says.

I pull them into the lift and activate for Deck A. "You know gossip and rumors can get you into trouble." *And me.* I eye Francesca who closes her eyes.

When we reach Deck A, there's that ghastly aroma of recycling: urine tanks, feces mulching, food decomposition, and medical decontamination. I force myself not to make a face. I need to set a good example.

"Yuck," the young seamstress says. "Where are we?"

I pull Francesca with me down a gray corridor to the dungeon, the ship's jail, while keeping a watchful eye that the others follow. She's like the Pied Piper. People follow without asking questions. That further tugs at my guilt.

We reach a gray steel door, which opens to my implant. That makes me wonder if Captain Beluga might cancel my authorization once I'm inside. I push those thoughts aside and lead three fabricators and two seamstresses into the hold. When the gray door seals behind us, the recycling smell fades.

A second gray door opens. Sergeant Kyra Yost stands along the wall with her MTT weapon drawn. The Multi-Tasking Taser is capable of immobilizing each or all seven of us. Francesca presses herself against the wall as I nudge the fabricators forward.

"What's this all about?" the fabrication supervisor says. "I thought you'd give us answers."

I urge the two seamstresses toward Yost and turn to

the supervisor. "Captain's orders. There was a terror attack. Captain suspects Returners."

The fabricators look at each other. "What attack?" the supervisor asks.

"I'm sorry. Until we find the saboteurs, Captain wants you to wait down here."

"We're under arrest?"

"Detention, for your own good," I say. "We don't want anyone seeking vengeance, do we?"

"What about Earth?" the supervisor asks.

"Until we know—"

"That's bull."

"I'll check back later," I say.

The supervisor grabs my arm. Francesca intervenes. "Let go."

"You're working with her?" the supervisor asks Francesca

"We'll get to the bottom of this. Nina is right. I've heard a lot of anger this morning."

"It's all lies," the supervisor says. "Lies. You hear me."

I wait until Sergeant Yost has the Returners locked up and lead Francesca back down the gray corridor.

"What if Returners didn't do this?" she asks.

"Who then? If EggFusion fails, we're doomed. Who would want that?"

"Returners don't."

"Most, maybe," I say. "But that fabrication supervisor is pretty angry."

* * *

Nina Rekovic Private Log 2098-10-18/12:22 PM

We reach the last of the Returners, two couples from the Ag Facility, in the commons on level forty-eight. Several angry women corner them, yelling, "Traitors."

I have one hand on my stun gun, praying I don't have to use it. Seeing Francesca, the angry crowd turns on her. She joins the Ag workers to comfort them.

I stand where I can see them all. "Listen to me. Get back to your stations. Captain's orders: I'm taking these four to lockup."

"They've destroyed our future," Delilah Witherspoon says. The fiery redhead has caused me trouble before.

"I doubt Ag workers had anything to do with it. They don't have access." I don't mention that they could easily tamper with food to create havoc.

The redhead gets into my face. "You're one of them. That's why."

I've seen her get physical with other women, which has me wanting to step back, but I stand my ground. "You want a week in lockup?"

"Screw you." She turns to the other women. "Let them suffer with the recycling waste."

When Delilah leads her rabble away, I join Francesca and the Ag workers. "You okay?"

"Thanks," a pretty brunette says. "I thought they'd lynch us. Do we have to go to lockup? We promise to stay in our rooms. You could have us monitored."

"Captain's orders, for your own protection."

Francesca frowns.

"We didn't do anything," the brunette says.

"I believe you. Please come quietly."

Francesca nods and the Ag women comply.

After Sergeant Yost takes them to their cells, Francesca grabs my arm. "I'm staying to make sure they're okay. Find out what's going on, and watch your back."

"I need your help up there."

"I'd be a target and a distraction. Good luck."

* * *

Nina Rekovic Private Log 2098-10-18/3:08 PM

I've missed the entire day in engineering and haven't heard from Zola. I swing by to find the pinched-face blonde at my desk, getting too comfortable in my absence.

No time for jealousies.

"What have you learned?"

Zola jumps out of my seat and stands back. "Just keeping things going."

"And your report?"

"Captain stopped by and took it. She said not to distract you; that you were working on delicate, confidential business."

"What about your findings?" I try to contain my irritation.

"Right. Whoever did this knew enough about electronics to incapacitate the EFF units. They're fried."

"Can you rebuild them?"

My other Senior Engineer enters. "Hey, Zol—" Jen's tanned round face shows surprise framed by puffy black curls. She blushes and leaves, making me wonder what else is going on.

Later.

"Not sure," Zola says. "It was tricky equipment to begin with—eighty percent failure rates."

"What about the backup unit?"

"Also fried. Professional job."

"How soon can you determine if we can fix this?" I ask.

Zola moves away from my desk, toward the door. "I need a day or two to come up with a plan."

"Make sure I see it first."

She nods. "Will do, boss."

I head toward the fertility lab on twelve; have to see for myself. On my Eye-Pad I see clusters of women arguing. Using my wrist-com, I link the sound to my ear implants and hear them talk about the roundup of Returners and rumors about Earth.

Only the captain, Carmen, and I knew, and I told no one. This could get ugly if I don't figure out who's behind the sabotage and the leak. We should have told the passengers up front.

"Put them on a shuttle and send them home," a voice yells as I pass through the cafeteria. I turn to see the redhead. "Kick them off this ark."

"Kill them, in other words. Is that what we stand for?"

"They shouldn't have signed on."

"Some were tricked."

The redhead backs away when she sees I'm still operating as Security Chief with my hand on my stun gun. I can imagine what she'll say behind my back. Captain wants a troublemaker; I'd nominate her. I keep moving.

It's like high school, where I was odd girl out. I try to forget, but watching cliques, alliances, politicking, and back-stabbing brings back sour memories.

I'm surprised when I reach the fertility lab to find doors open and lights out. I activate the switch and try to close the doors. They're jammed.

Sergeant Wynona Tucker jumps out from one of the examination rooms with her stun gun out. Seeing me, the stocky cop puts it down. "Captain assigned me because we can't lock the facilities. They busted this place up good."

I'm annoyed that Zola didn't mention the damage and Captain Beluga didn't inform me she was assigning my security team. "What have you learned?"

Tucker resets a silent alarm at the door. "Someone came in last night after the lab was locked. It looks to me like someone on the inside."

"Why do you say that?"

"Door wasn't forced. It was damaged after, to make it look like a break-in. They cut circuits to the lab and pulsed the equipment. That fried everything except the lights, which are on a different circuit." More that wasn't in Zola's brief report.

"What about cams?" I ask.

"Nothing."

"Erased?"

"No," Tucker says. "Timestamp shows no gaps and no activity. Whoever did this was well-informed and clever."

"So we're looking at someone who works in the lab,

has access to our secured pulse weapons, and can tamper with the cams."

The sergeant nods and pushes back strands of brown hair.

"I don't suppose we have any real suspects."

"No, but it has to be someone who wants us to turn back."

"Keep digging. Next time give me a courtesy message that you've been assigned."

"Will do."

* * *

Nina Rekovic Private Log 2098-10-18/6:02 PM

What troubles me about the timing of the attack, after rumors spread about Earth, is that a non-Returner might have changed her mind. Anyone can be a suspect. I track Carmen to Crazy Eights Bar on level eight.

How original.

When I get there, she's plastered, as much as you can be on two percent alcohol and sedatives. I've never seen her this bad.

"Time to go home," I tell her.

"You don't own me."

That's the bone we keep fighting over. While we've lived together for six years and she's the reason I came, she never wanted a commitment.

I rub her shoulders. "You should get some sleep."

Carmen pulls away. "Enough."

"Can we go talk somewhere?"

"You should move out."

That stings and draws attention from patrons who suddenly look alert and sober.

"I miss you," I whisper.

"Hey, you heard our friend," a crusty brunette yells. "Buzz off. You're spoiling our fun."

"Not so tough off the job." It's the redhead, Delilah. "Hey, everyone, our chief cop is a Returner sympathizer."

"I'm a peace officer," I say.

"Maybe you're the saboteur. After all, you have access to everything and you're friendly with Returners."

"Why don't you all go sleep this off?"

"Why don't you step outside?" The redhead stands before me with almost masculine features.

I look to Carmen, who in the past has stood by me. She stares at the counter and takes another drink. I signal Sergeants Yost and Tucker, leaving my com open. "One more word and I'll close Crazy Eights for the night and send the speaker down to Deck A."

I back up toward the door, making sure no one is behind me. It's something I've noticed over the past few months, something that crept up on me. A few of the women, the redhead in particular, have taken on aggressive masculine behavior.

Nature abhors a vacuum.

* * *

Nina Rekovic Private Log 2098-10-18/7:13 PM

While I make my way down teal corridors to my apartment, I scan my Eye-Pad for other bar activity. Looks like the sabotage and rumors of Earth have everyone on edge. I'll have to ask the captain for more security if this keeps up. But there are few I'd trust. Francesca is in lockup and Carmen isn't talking to me. Issues with my roommate/partner—I'm not sure which—have been brewing for some time. I can't keep ignoring them.

Absent her, I'm a Returner. But sabotage isn't the answer.

The Maiden's Ark is a fragile vessel despite the best technology Captain McDonald could buy. It reminds me of the Titanic, the unsinkable vessel until it wasn't. The fertility sabotage was a blow, a wake-up call that internal conflict could doom us. It's hard enough to get a dozen people to work together let alone a quarter million, yet we have to settle our differences peacefully. And, we have to go back for the sake of the human race, to help survivors, and because ignoring their plight diminishes us as human beings.

My implant triggers my apartment door to open. I go in before I realize I'm not alone. The short, sixteen-year-old blonde who trails after me is Zola's reclusive daughter, Magdalena. When the blonde closes the door, my first paranoid thought is I shouldn't be alone with her.

It's a trap.

She plops her agile form on the worn love seat in the corner of my living room. She acts bouncy like the puppy I had to give up when I came aboard.

"You should deputize me as your private detective," she says with a gleam in her eye that has me curious.

"Shouldn't you be home with your mom?"

"She's too busy hopping into bed with Jen."

Magdalena doesn't need this and I certainly don't need to know my two Senior Engineers are shacking up.

"I'm sorry," I say. "Do you have something to tell me?"

She hops up and examines a picture on the end table of me and my dad before he died. "Swear me in as your private detective and I'll help you catch the saboteur. Did I say that right?"

I nod. "You're too young. Your mother would never approve."

"That's why we need a secret ceremony."

She has my attention. I won't ask her to do anything risky, so I play along. "Raise your right hand and repeat after me. I, Magdalena Cohen swear to obey all orders given to me by Nina Rekovic as Chief of Security."

She so swears.

"So what's on your mind?"

"I know you're sympathetic to Returners even though you rounded them up. Well, I'm a Returner. Whew, I've never told anyone before, except Mom."

"You shouldn't be telling me."

"But you just deputized me."

I want to slap my head. *Keep playing along.* "Okay."

"The other girls ignore me 'cause I'm quiet, but I see everything." She plops back on the love seat, but she's too restless. "Returners didn't break into the fertility lab."

"You have evidence?"

"I just know."

"That's not good enough," I say. "You want something to drink?" I pour myself a Dream Drifter to help me forget about Carmen and fall into a deep slumber.

"Mom says I'm too young for that. I tried it once. It doesn't work for me."

I push the glass aside. "You shouldn't be—" I catch myself. I'm not her mom and she should be going. I nudge her toward the door.

Magdalena stops me before I open the door. "You shouldn't drink that junk, either. It can mess up your mind. I'll keep my eyes open for you."

"Don't get into trouble."

"Thanks. Give me a signal and I'll be there for you." She gives me a hug; then rushes out.

I return to my Dream Drifter and stare at the pale blue liquid. I've been relying too much on this. Has it dulled my senses?

* * *

Nina Rekovic Private Log 2098-10-19/8:33 AM

Carmen didn't come home again last night. When I reach the orange com-room on my morning rounds, she's gone. I do Eye-Pad scans of common areas; see more clusters, more whispering about Earth and sabotage. What I don't see are any officers. I check the engineering unit, and can't find Zola. *That's odd.*

Checking past cam history, I see why. All department heads except me have assembled in the captain's conference room. Zola is there in my absence. I check my wrist-com for missed communications. No messages except a cryptic: Eye C 26-Com. *Another crank note?*

I reach the conference room as the door slides open.

Department heads rush past me like I'm invisible. I stop Zola. "Why wasn't I invited?" I whisper.

"Talk to the captain."

I enter the conference room to find Captain Beluga and Carmen whispering in the corner. I strain to hear; they stop.

"Close the door," the captain says, which triggers the door to shut by itself.

"Why wasn't I invited?" I ask. "And don't say because I was asleep."

"Always direct. Very well, I've gotten reports that you sympathize with Returners."

"What evidence?" I ask.

"Confidential sources."

"As the ship's peace officer, I get people to talk instead of letting frustrations simmer. That's all."

Beluga approaches me. "This is a serious threat. I have to ask you to step down as Chief of Security."

"You use me to round up Returners, and then strip me of the title."

"I am removing you from security entirely. Carmen will take your place."

"I'm still Chief Engineer," I say, "unless you're taking that as well."

"Evidence points to three Returners sabotaging our fertility lab. Until I complete my investigation, I don't want you involved. You'll confine yourself to Engineering until further notice."

"Does that mean you're releasing the other Returners?"

"Not until things settle down."

I know Carmen turned the captain against me, but confronting her won't help. All I can do is stew as I leave the conference room. Unable to face my engineering duties, I head to the commons, wondering what evidence Captain Beluga could have. I know she tracks my movements. I don't think I said anything compromising.

Then I recall Magdalena.

I check last night's cam footage of the hallway outside my apartment. Carmen carries a suitcase from our apartment to the captain's quarters. Shaking, I clench my fists.

Carmen and Beluga?

I force myself to breathe, and detour away from the commons. Last thing I need is to run into anyone. Using my Eye-Pad, I find clear lifts and corridors back toward my apartment to freshen up. Returning to last night's cam recordings, I fast forward to when I came home.

Watching myself stroll toward the apartment, I wait for the moment Magdalena jumped out of the shadows. I reached the door. It opened. I went in. No Magdalena.

Was she already in the apartment? Having traced from when Carmen left to when I got home heightens my anxiety. Did Carmen let her in? Is Magdalena part of this? Her mom was at the meeting.

When I reach the apartment, I go in, expecting Magdalena to leap out again. She doesn't. I go the fridge for something to drink and find the glass of Dream Drifter where I placed it. It's black with writhing threads, parasites.

Magdalena?

I wish I had cam footage of last night inside the apartment. To the best of my knowledge that doesn't exist. Staring at the drink, I can almost feel those filaments entering my brain, leading to madness. I've seen its effects. Then I recall Magdalena telling me not to drink. Was she warning me? Did she know?

I check the message again: Eye C 26-Com. Of course, Icy is a nickname people gave me when I joined Maiden's Ark. I wasn't outgoing like Carmen. I kept to myself like Magdalena does.

On my Eye-Pad I check the commons on deck twenty-six, and find clusters of women gossiping. I listen in and hear concerns about our rumors. I check the timestamp for the message and scan cam history. Sergeant Yost was up from lockup talking with Senior Engineer Zola Cohen, Magdalena's mom. Ordinarily I wouldn't give it another thought. I listen and have to run the sound track through filters to make sense of the whispering.

"I've had no sympathy for Returners until now," Zola says. "I'm concerned about Earth survivors as well. But I don't want to lose my daughter over this."

"Can you get a message to the counsel?" Yost asks.

"I'll try."

"We need a ship-wide vote. Let the people decide."

"Captain won't allow it. She called a meeting this morning to remove Nina from security and the investigation."

The two women slipped away, just another gossip corner on the ship. How many others are sympathetic yet afraid to speak out?

It's time to choose sides, but either way, I betray people I care about. I don't want to turn this into a conflict where everyone loses. I have friends on both sides. At least I thought I did. This could become as contentious as when we embarked on this voyage against government and public protests.

I check my face. It looks like I haven't slept in weeks. Shrugging, I make my way back to the captain's office. On the way, I go to erase the Eye C message. I can't find it. I return to the video of Zola and Yost, and find the commons empty with the time-stamp of when they were there. I even see a plate on a nearby table that was there, but no Zola or Yost.

Did I imagine that?

It's probably a trap, but I enter the captain's office anyway. She already suspects me of being a Returner, might as well take a stand.

"I've been expecting you." Captain Beluga's big frame towers over me. "Sit."

I pace instead. "I don't believe I've ever given you cause to question my loyalty."

"Just being cautious."

"I gather Carmen is with you now."

The captain sits behind her large mahogany desk, something she brought from her corporate offices on Earth. "What was it you were saying about loyalty?"

"Mine is to you and everyone on the Maiden's Ark."

"I'm confused. You keep changing subjects."

Confused, yes. Changing subjects, no.

"You and Carmen betrayed my trust by hooking up. I can accept that. What I can't accept is pushing our small community into civil war."

Captain Beluga's eyes narrow. "What are you getting at?"

"You had me imprison those Returners who were outspoken before we heard about Earth. There are many more now."

"Give me names. We'll deal with them."

"I'm no longer in security, remember. Besides, I have reason to believe after hearing about Earth that the majority of the passengers and crew want to return."

That blow seems to hit the captain hard, but she recovers. "We're not turning around."

"I support your mission, Captain, but I think for the sake of peace, that we should put this to a vote. Let both sides make their case and let the majority decide."

"This is not a democracy."

"I know, Captain. I seek to avoid conflict that will tear us apart."

"Giving Returners a forum will do exactly that. This conversation is over."

* * *

Nina Rekovic Private Log 2098-10-19/1:42 PM

Unable to concentrate on my engineering duties, I drop down to Deck A to visit Francesca. Sergeant Yost won't let me enter the gray corridor leading to the jail cells. I'm tempted to bring up her meeting with Zola, but I don't want to out them.

Agitated, I return to engineering. I haven't seen Zola since she left the captain's meeting. She's probably running my investigation now. Instead, I find round-faced Senior Engineer Jen Adams, Zola's new lover. She's also one of Beluga's faithful, but I'm not sure where else to turn.

"Let's say, hypothetically, that we wanted to do a ship-wide vote, how could we do that?"

Her dark, tanned face is a mask, even as her eyes tighten, studying me. "Don't pull me into one of your schemes."

"When have I ever asked you to do anything that wasn't in the best interests of the crew and passengers?"

Jen starts counting off on her fingers, but says nothing.

"That's what I thought. Now humor me."

"I'll have to report this to the captain," Jen says.

"Report what? That I've asked you a hypothetical question?"

"You're up to something. Okay, assuming you alert everyone, they can respond giving their DNA prints on their wrist-coms. But returning will jeopardize our goals."

"Why not let the people decide?" I ask.

"I can't do that without captain's approval. She won't give it."

My Eye-Pad shows four newly deputized guards in uniform heading for engineering, for me. And they can track me.

"Jen, let me put this to the passengers. I promise to abide by their decision either way."

"I'm sorry, Chief. I can't."

"Then cover for me."

I hurry out of engineering, heading away from the four deputized guards. I don't fancy joining the other Returners on Deck A. I track the guards. While figuring where to go, I notice something strange on my Eye-com. It shows Magdalena walking next to me. But when I look around, I'm alone. The image disappears.

How did you do that?

Taking the lift up a deck, I move toward the commons lifts. I follow a faint line on the Eye-Pad that's not on the actual yellow nano-polymer floors. When I look for the guards, they're running around the engineering deck, bumping into each other. They've lost my signal.

Well, my deputized assistant, if this is your doing, I guess I owe you. I expect to take the lift to level twenty-six commons, but instead find myself on level eight, heading for Crazy Eights. It's the last place I want to go, especially when I find Carmen slumped at the bar.

I stand next to her and look at her ratty, shoulder-length brown hair. Horrible hair day. "Your back-stabbing might win you points with the captain, but everyone else should know what you are."

Carmen stands to confront me, but she's had too much Sedate Living to muster anger. *Feeling guilty, are you?*

I've never seen Carmen this wasted and wonder if Beluga pressured her to cheat on me. I push her back into her seat. "I don't want you back when this is over." I feel sorry for her when she slumps into her seat. Her eyes look up, pleading.

On my Eye-Pad, I see guards regroup and head for the lift. It didn't take long for someone to rat me out. The redhead, Delilah, stands by the door tapping on her E-Notepad. I grab the unit and drop it onto a yellow table, too bright for a bar.

I stand back in case she gets physical. "Why don't you and I air our grievances before whoever will listen. After all, we're too small a community to let this conflict simmer." I hope my deputized assistant can get this onto the intercom feed. I hear an echo from the blue corridor outside. The doors close.

Clever girl.

"I challenge you to debate here and now whether we should return to Earth and help survivors rebuild or continue along our way."

"You're nuts," the redhead says. "There's nothing to debate. We're not turning back."

"You're afraid?"

"You're on." The redhead stands aside so she can face her audience in the bar. "Everyone on this ship signed a contract to follow the captain and abide by her charter to start a new civilization. Everyone knew there was no going back. Yet, Returner-traitors had second thoughts. Too bad."

"That was before we got bad news about Earth," I say.

"Doesn't matter. Returning wastes valuable fuel and resources that will jeopardize our future. For what? A few thousand men on the moon base. Boo-hoo. We've sacrificed too much to get this far. Our future is forward, not back. We can't waste our prospects because they squandered theirs."

"We can't hold them accountable for this natural disaster."

"Maybe not," Delilah says, picking up her E-Notepad. "But if we turn back now, it'll take over five years to return. Chances of finding survivors is nil, none. Then we'd have wasted time and resources for nothing. It's triage. We have a better chance without them. Besides, from the beginning of time men have oppressed us. I will not give them another chance."

"You're afraid we'll have to bring them with us."

"Exactly. They'll never be able to sustain a civilization on the moon without Earth."

"Yet, we have for five years and expect to for generations." I check my Eye-Pad. Guards have reached the blue corridor outside Crazy Eights. They can't open the doors. *Thanks, special assistant.*

"Only if we don't squander what we have," Delilah says.

"All you say is true. It's not without risks."

Delilah grins. "Then you concede the debate."

"I would have before we learned that two asteroids collided into Earth." I say this to clear up rumors. "It's like what wiped out the dinosaurs. Only the moon base and asteroid miners have survived. They need our help."

"None of that changes the facts," Delilah says.

"The covenant and all decisions we've agreed to up until now were before we got this news. Our ship is the last hope of humans, here and back there."

"So let's create our new civilization, based on new values."

"If we don't return," I say. "We doom everyone left back home. The lunar base can't survive without resupply. We don't have to bring them onto the Ark. We can help them become self-sufficient. Then we can continue our mission knowing we've done our best."

"We'd lose over ten years for a lost cause."

"There's another reason to go back. I believe we can fix our EggFusion process. However, should the delicate system fail in future, we doom humankind by not leaving an alternative."

"We need to make sure it doesn't fail by keeping Returners away from it," Delilah says. "You've offered nothing convincing."

"Then try this. Returning is the compassionate alternative, the moral choice, the best chance for the survival of the human race. We value compassion. Yet when called, we turn our backs. Our new civilization is built on principles of helping fellow humans. If we fail now, then we give lie to principles that inspired us on this journey. All arguments against return given this new information are based on selfish considerations."

My Eye-Pad shows the guards have brought Jen to help pry open the door to Crazy Eights.

"I call upon all crew and passengers on the Maiden's Ark. Vote your conscience. Let the captain know where you stand. I'll abide by the will of the people."

"Bold words," Delilah says. "But you're going to jail.

Hope you enjoy cleaning recycling tanks."

The captain joins the guards and Jen trying to force the door.

"I cast my vote for return," I say. "Everyone please cast yours. Then abide by the results. We cannot continue to fight among ourselves and expect our new society to flourish."

"Oh, shut up." Carmen pushes me away from Delilah's E-Notepad. "What's all this fuss?"

I grab the E-Notepad. "I've had enough of you. You betrayed me by sleeping with the Captain and turning on me like a rabid dog. That's not how you treat your partner."

Zola arrives outside and gets the door open. Six deputized guards in uniform rush in followed by the captain, who towers over them.

"Arrest her," Beluga says.

"You might want to look at the results first." I hold up Delilah's E-Notepad. "Eighty percent in favor of return, with over forty percent voting."

"Numbers mean nothing," the captain says.

"They mean people are upset and you're not listening. In fact I now have evidence that you sabotaged the fertility lab so you could blame Returners before they could lobby for return."

The captain turns to Zola. "Turn off the loudspeaker."

Zola shakes her head. "I stand with the people, Captain. Did you sabotage the lab?"

"All lies." Captain McDaniels turns to the guards. "Arrest them both, for sedition."

"Are you sure you want to imprison eighty percent of the passengers and crew? That's not what we signed up for."

When the guards hesitate, the captain turns to Sergeant Tucker. "I promote you to Chief of Security. Arrest these two and anyone who acts treasonous."

Sergeant Tucker clears her throat. "Then I place you

under arrest for sabotaging the fertility lab and trumping up charges to arrest Returners."

"You can't arrest me," Captain McDaniels says. "This is my ship."

"You just gave me the authority to arrest traitors."

* * *

Nina Rekovic Private Log 2098-10-19/2:49 PM

As new Chief of Security, Tucker releases the Returners from their cells on Deck A and adds two new occupants, Captain McDaniels and Senior Engineer Jen Adams. By popular acclaim and experience, the executive officers name Delilah Witherspoon to captain the ship during the trip back, despite her resistance to going back. Francesca returns to managing our meals.

Slowing, turning around, and speeding toward Earth takes over a month, but when the final results of the second poll come back, over ninety-five percent of the crew and passengers agree it's the right thing to do.

While I avoid Crazy Eights, I see Carmen from time to time. She begs me to take her back and forgive her for bending to Beluga's will. I might have considered how she fell under our captain's power, but I can't forgive those tiny black worms in my Dream Drifter. I send that through hazmat disposal. Based on the evidence, Carmen joins the captain in a separate cell on Deck A.

It takes a month, but Zola gets the fertility lab working. It would have taken longer, but she pours her own betrayal at the hands of her lover, Jen, into fixing what Jen destroyed.

That leaves Magdalena without parental supervision. While I look after her, she teaches me the fine points of 3D chess and helps me get through Carmen's betrayal.

One thing still troubles me. "How did you know my drink was contaminated?"

Magdalena grins. "People think I'm slow because I don't talk much. The captain gave Carmen something that she held at arm's length like poison. Yet, she brought it home."

"I owe you many thanks. We all do."

"I'm scared about going back." Magdalena looks down.

"Then why—"

"I hated Jen so much I thought going back would make things better. It won't, will it?"

I shake my head. "No, but we'll manage."

OTHER STORIES BY LANCE ERLICK

THE REBEL WITHIN (Rebel Series book 1)

After another U.S. civil war, a different kind of rebel arises. Annabelle (16) lives in a world where men are exiled, quarantined or forced to fight to the death to train the military elite. Encountering a male escapee, the only safe course for her as cop intern is to turn him in. Instead, she risks everything to spare the boy from his fate, even as she's forced into this elite military.

THE REBEL TRAP (Rebel Series book 2)

Voices in 16-year-old Annabelle's head aren't God or signs she's going mad—yet. Thanks to auditory implants and cams, her military commander from the unit that took her parents watches her 24-7. She's forced to be a cop and military spy investigating her police captain. She's caught between the commander who pushes for results, the captain who baits her, and a boy who hacks her implants and tugs at her to help his brother escape.

REBELS DIVIDED (Rebel Series book 3)

The first time they saw each other, they met as enemies and she didn't shoot him. That counted for something.

After the Second American Civil War, a nation divided. A young man and woman from enemy camps must come together to rescue her sister and gain justice for his pa's murder. Complicating this, the Federal Governor and Outland warlord conclude a secret deal, pledging her in marriage to the warlord and putting a bounty on the young man. While trying to survive and achieve their goals, the pair must struggle with growing feelings for each other despite being sworn enemies.

WATCHING YOU (short story)

At the intersection of global tracking, pervasive networks, mass storage, and the Patriot Act, we have the ability and some say the obligation to know everything about everyone. Can privacy survive? Can the individual endure?

ABOUT THE AUTHOR

Lance Erlick grew up in various parts of the United States and Europe. He took to stories as his anchor and was inspired by his father's engineering work on cutting-edge aerospace projects to look to the future. He writes science fiction, dystopian and young adult fiction, and likes to explore the future implications of social and technological trends. He is the author of *The Rebel Within*, *The Rebel Trap*, and *Rebels Divided*, three books in the Rebel series. In those stories, he flips traditional exploitation to explore the effects of a world that discriminates against males and the consequences of following conscience for those coming of age.

Find out more about the author and his work at LanceErlick.com. Go to that website to sign up to receive occasional email newsletters with links to free short stories, and updates on new releases and other writing developments.